USBORNE FIRST READING
Level Two

Old Mother Hubbard

Retold by Russell Punter
Illustrated by Fred Blunt

The Genie in the Bottle

Retold by Rosie Dickins
Illustrated by Sara Rojo

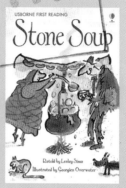

Stone Soup

Retold by Lesley Sims
Illustrated by Georgien Overwater

The Baobab Tree

Retold by Louie Stowell
Illustrated by Laure Fournier

The Old Woman who lived in a Shoe

Retold by Russell Punter
Illustrated by Joelle Dreidemy

USBORNE YOUNG READING

The Little Giraffe

Retold by Lesley Sims
Illustrated by Laure Fournier

Clever Rabbit and the Lion

Retold by Susanna Davidson
Illustrated by Daniel Howarth

Brer Rabbit and the Blackberry Bush

Retold by

The Chilly Little Penguin

...ter
...hen Galbis

Little Miss Muffet

Retold by Russell Punter

Illustrated by Lorena Alvarez

Reading consultant: Alison Kelly
Roehampton University

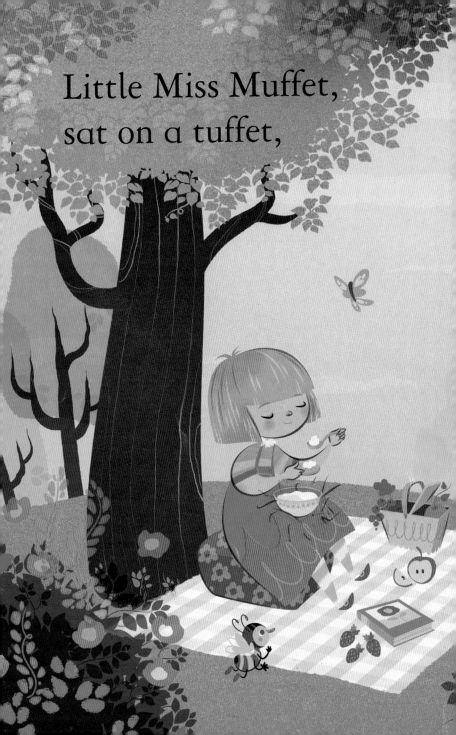

Little Miss Muffet,
sat on a tuffet,

eating her curds
and whey.

Along came a
spider,

who dropped down
beside her

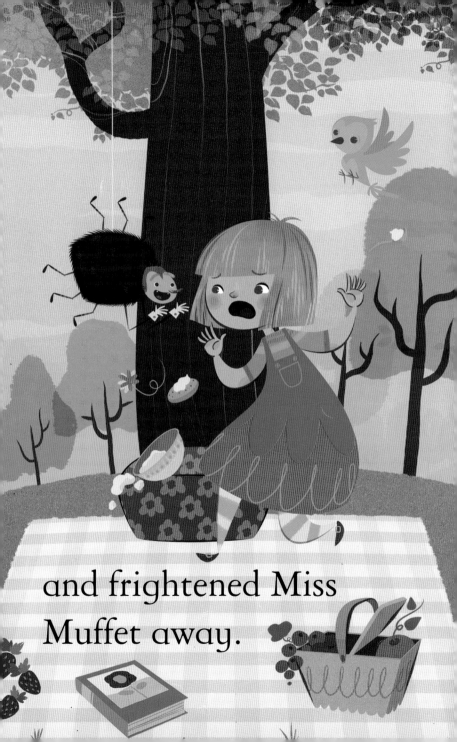

and frightened Miss
Muffet away.

"Help!" cried
Miss Muffet.

She ran from her tuffet

and into the woods
down below.

"Come back!" called
the spider.

He rushed off
to find her.

"I'm sorry for scaring
you so."

The little girl sighed.

"What a bad place to hide."

Then she heard
a deep growl

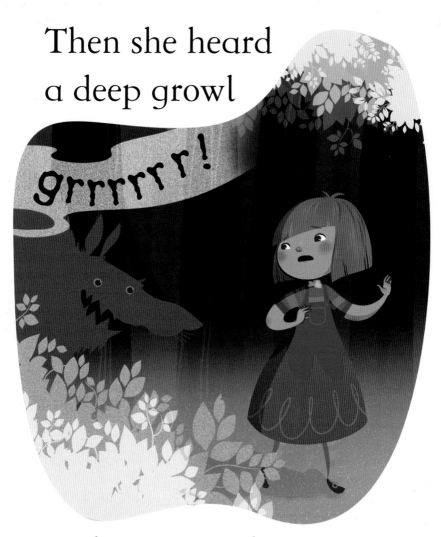

grrrrrr!

and an ear-splitting
howl.

OWWWOOOOO!

They gave poor Miss
Muffet a fright.

A big wolf jumped out.
He said with a shout,

"It's time for my dinner,
my dear."

"I'll have little girl pie!"

"Put her down!" came
a cry.

"Don't worry –
Seb Spider is here."

The wolf gave a smile. "I do like your style.

But what can you do against me?"

"I'll show you," said Seb.

He spun a strong web

and tied the bad wolf
to a tree.

Miss Muffet said, "Seb, what a wonderful web.

Now let's go!"

So Seb showed
her the way.

Now she's friends with
Seb Spider.

He hangs down
beside her

and spins for Miss
Muffet all day.

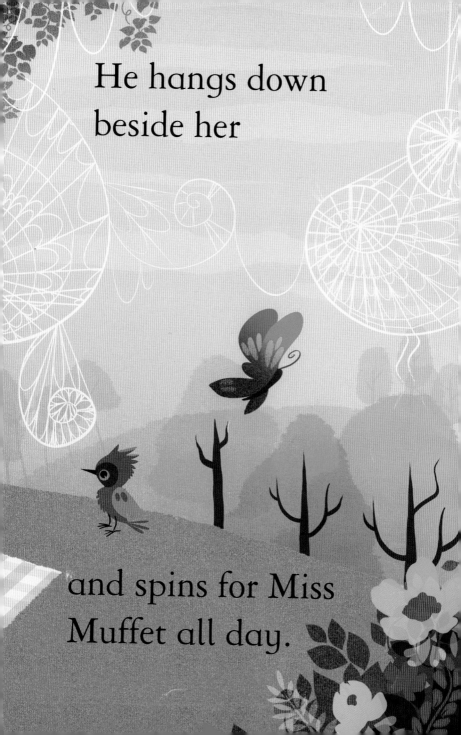

PUZZLES

Puzzle 1

Can you spot the differences between these two pictures? There are six to find.

Puzzle 2
Find these things in
the picture:

spider　　book　　tree

web　　girl　　bird

Puzzle 3
Choose the best speech bubble for each picture.

Answers to puzzles

Puzzle 1

Puzzle 2

tree spider web

web

girl book bird

Puzzle 3

Come back!

Put her down!

About the rhyme

The original version of *Little Miss Muffet* first appeared in print over two hundred years ago.

Curd is thickened milk used to make cheese. Whey is a watery liquid made when the milk is thickened.

Series editor: Lesley Sims

First published in 2012 by Usborne Publishing Ltd., Usborne House, 83-85 Saffron Hill, London EC1N 8RT, England. www.usborne.com
Copyright © 2012 Usborne Publishing Ltd.

USBORNE FIRST READING
Level Three